secret
sermons

contemporary
contradictory
christian
poetry & prose

by victoria hope petersen

Secret Sermons:
Contemporary Contradictory Christian Poetry &
Prose

ISBN: 9781729314074

to jacob – these poems were published because you insisted they are worth reading and because you have always insisted that i am worthy. thank you for reminding me of God's love daily and pushing me to organize the words in my journal and on my social media into something that makes me proud. i love you.

to Jesus Christ – may He receive all of the glory for any inspiration, joy, peace, or goodness anyone finds from these words. He is the author of my very blessed life.

contents:

it is difficult to be human and flesh and spiritual and holy. not many Christians talk about the strain one suffers through while being both human and godly. the intention of these poems is to express that tension. to help humans better understand who we are, because we understand ourselves better the more we understand the God within us. and it is difficult to understand ourselves when we are only contradictions of what we desire to be and what we are supposed to be. these poems were inspired by joys, sorrows, lovers, heartbreaks, families while growing up in foster care, scriptures, and the healing and love of God.

scripture is God's "love letters" to us. it is through scripture God concretely communicates in a language we can translate and understand to tell us He loves us and what He loves about us. through scripture God explicitly gives us stories, illustrations, and depictions of what He has done to demonstrate His love for us. and some may ask the question "well, what about the parts where God tells us what to do that isn't necessarily convenient or pleasing to me?" God wants you and me to live the most beautiful and joy filled lives. it is through doing His will we come to understand and experience this beauty and joy He has for us. He grants us instruction as a gift so we may live a life experiencing crazy, enduring, and steadfast Love.

my hope is that you connect to my words, but not to connect to me - to connect to God and who He is and who He so desperately wants to be for you, because He wants to be known and loved by you as much as He knows and loves you.

"All Scripture is God-breathed and is useful for teaching, rebuking, correcting and training in righteousness" 2 Timothy 3:16.

His crucifixion & my heartbreak

though my middle name is "hope"
although people have spoken
this word over me
following a word
that means victory
my entire life
i've never felt more hopeless.
i've never felt more defeated.

*Be strong and take heart, all you who hope in the
LORD. Psalm 31:24*

why are you so terse with me?
i'm just trying to talk to you.
i'm your daughter.
why is the only time
you talk to me
is to point out
something i did wrong,
when i was trying to help
and do something right?
why am i such a disappointment?
why have i always been
a disappointment?

"how are you feeling," he asks.
"so good" i say.
this is all my response ever will be,
because i'd rather lie
everyday,
than watch you
walk away.

i cried out
as loud as a newborn
coming into earth
out of the womb.
i don't want any of you
inside of my womb.
begging you to stop
hurting me,
coming into me.
so you pushed my head
into the pillow.
you always knew
how to silence me.
you oppressed me
like a refugee.
and said "suck it up."
i always sucked you up.
and you will weep
someday
when you realize
what you did to me
after all i did for you.

i am not giving up.
i will not give up on you.
because love is patient.
so i will patiently
wait for you to change.
and love is kind.
so i will kindly speak to you
after you call me names.
love is not boastful.
so i will not point out
all of the sacrifices i make for you.
love holds no records of wrongs.
so i will forget about that time
you pushed me and that other time too.
love rejoices in the truth.
so i will continue to believe, at the perfect timing,
God will make you a new creation.
love always hopes.
so i will continue to pray for our relationship
and your heart's restoration.
love always endures.
so i will not give up on you.
i will never give up.

through the looking glass,
but what am i looking at?
like alice, i vowed to be a good friend
on this adventure.
i am devoted,
but this glass is broken.
please stop cutting me with it.
we can put it back together.
we can see what was supposed to be forever.
i can continue on this journey.
i'll fight any jabowakee for you.
but please,
i'm on my knees.
just stop hurting me.

why are all of the men
in my life
so damn mean?
even the words are similar.
men.
mean.
did someone all knowing
do that on purpose?

she was a rose
and they picked her.
not for a life with her.
just to watch her wither.

i thank God you finally left.
because i could not leave you.
i was ready to end it.
it being my own life.
i was ready to leave myself.

man could have never saved me
even if he tried.
he was weak
like the rest of them.
like my father
and my father's father.

thanks for being nice.
it's been years now.
it's just the way people talk to me.
and it feels like
i'm being cut with a knife.
words as cold as ice.
even after a sacred vow,
he started to talk to me like
all those other men
filled with hatred and strife.

monsters raise monsters.
and i will not allow
a fiend to be a part of my life
or the life
i will someday create.

it is unfortunate not for my sake,
but yours.
i could have made you a deal
with the best drug.
if you would have never
left.
i'm the best plug.
if you would have just
stayed
long enough
for the high.
i am ecstasy.
but you were addicted to everything
except my love.

when i lay in bed at night
i think of what you did
before you lied in bed at night.
you lied
for two years
to my face.
and when i lay in bed
i picture your face
as you watched another woman
on a screen
fake it.
a woman who was sold
unwillingly into an industry
that took her life away,
that leaves her empty.
you left me empty.
i have never felt so alone
as i did
when i was with you.
i didn't even have myself
because you stripped me
of myself.
at first my clothes.
but when i turned that to a close,
you stripped me of
who God created me to be.
i pray for you now.
that God uses this
to form you into the man
you were meant to be.
and i thank God
you weren't meant to be
mine.

because of all of the men
that have left me behind,
none of them have hurt me
as much as you.
especially when you shoved
yourself inside of me,
as if you were trying
to dig something out.
you dug out
trauma and memories.
because when i asked you
to be gentle,
to go slow,
to show me love,
you'd get mad.
you were the angriest human
i've ever encountered.
and you'll never admit
all i tried to do
was love you
unconditionally through.
or maybe someday you'll admit
you couldn't love me
because you loved the fake scream
of the sad lady on the tv.
the truth was not evident
because you lived a lie
you still live behind.
and for so long we hid together
behind aesthetic instagram pictures
and fake laughter at parties.
i was manipulating the people to see
what i wanted them to see.

you always said i was manipulative.
but did you never notice
how you manipulated me?
so you could sit in front of the screen
to watch the same scenes
my uncle had me watch
before he chose to rape me.
you broke me.
and sometimes i want to tell you
i hate you.
but that is a lie.
because i love you.
for all that you did for me.
when you ignored me,
you made me tough.
when you criticized me
you made me more self-aware.
when you made me sit alone,
i drew closer to God
when i lied in my bed
knowing we were living a lie
my faith strengthened,
as i remembered God's promises.
that i was meant to live for Him,
and i was meant to love you
so you could love
someone else better
than you ever loved me.

i love too much
and hurt,
because God loved so much
and hurt.

mini sermon: yourself as a new creation

that year left me feeling defeated and destroyed. i was in the unhealthiest relationship i have ever been in and it took me away from everything good in my life. i lost most of my close relationships. i spent many days in tears and sleeping. spending time with God was solely me begging Him to give me direction even though i knew what way to go.

throughout the entire school year i knew God was calling me home for the summer. regardless of the other offers i received for other internships and jobs around the globe, i knew i had to find an opportunity at home. thankfully, so thankfully, my church gave me that opportunity. i was ready for a summer revolved around my family, Christ, and healing myself through His strength and love.

on my missions trip to peru, i encountered a cross made from scraps and debris of buildings and architecture terrorists had bombed and destroyed in war. the people of the country came together and created something to depict and glorify Christ out of ruins.

i knew God was calling me home for a few different reasons – restoration and healing - but i have learned He was calling me home for many other purposes i would have never expected or even imagined. i am absolutely sure He called me home for more than i can understand.

God makes broken things beautiful in the most awe inspiring way; and i am so grateful for that miserable school year and beautiful summer. everything each of them brought - the lessons, the realizations, the relationships, the growth, more pain and suffering, but more love for God, as i understood the pain and suffering He endured was much worse.

you may be the most broken you have ever been, but i promise, it is in the unknowing, in the trials and in the trusting of God's love, the unimaginable and unpredictable opportunities are made possible. so keep holding on. and thank God for whatever destroyed you, because you're alive and He is an artist, who can make anything new. you must believe in Him. you are a new creation.

2 Corinthians 5:17
Therefore, if anyone is in Christ, he is a new creature; the old things passed away; behold, new things have come.

attempted & half-witted reconciliation

i've learned seeing as much good in myself
as i do in others is acceptable.
i've learned love without boundaries is slavery.
i've learned my beliefs drive my actions in such a
radical
yet beautiful way.
i've learned that i like taking care of myself
as much as i like taking care of others.
i've learned my strengths
can outweigh my weaknesses.
i've learned that loving myself
is just as important as loving my neighbor.

like my father should have
you held me
as if you were never
going to let go.

they say i need to be complete
all by myself.
whole and perfect,
able to present myself neat,
new merchandise on a shelf.
but the truth is
i find myself broken
i pick and prod
and can convince myself
to hate what is within.
but our relationship is healing.
such an overwhelming feeling.

-dependence

i want to know you.
let me dive into your heart.
swimming and exploring
the beautiful ocean
that is this amazing man
i love.
tell me more about you
because i cannot wait until
we are in person
to be drenched in you.
not because you don't give enough.
because i can't get enough.

spring came back
to make love with fall.
she whispered to him,
"no matter how dead you become,
i will choose to see your color."
she created beauty in his decay
brightened his rainy day
with her sunny haze.
his leaves cried
as winter and summer proclaimed them
as the most beautiful day.

i want you to kiss me
like the warm and light
raindrops.
i want your touch
to be like this soft mist
covering my skin.

you are the smell of
misty rain
and you taste
of the shining sun.
so my legs spread
as flowers bloom.

-painful mistakes

you cannot save me.
i don't want you to save me.
so how do you continually
end up saving me?

as a woman
i will not be chastened
for having sexual desires.
i will not glorify virgins for their purity,
and i will not shame other women for not saving
themselves for marriage,
because i know how much it hurts
to intentionally give yourself to another
human being.
in the present,
in the moment,
as my body is telling the truth.
i am committed.
i want to be one with him.
i am sure.
this is the purest promise
i have made.
yet my hands are the dirtiest
they have even been
after he unexpectedly leaves
after this vow.
and my spirit questions why
my body lied.
this is a mystery to me,
for i made a pledge to take care
of his body for a lifetime.
and i would have never broken it
if he just would have given me the chance.
i keep all promises.
with my spirit, mind, and
body.
i will not humiliate another beautiful
and beloved,

because someone did not delight in her
the way God intended.
this action takes two.
and i know she is already
feeling as i felt
after closing my legs
to another man who lied
before closing his arms,
mind,
and heart
to all i had to offer.

-an effort to use powerful and lying words in
powerless and lying moments

i do not believe in soulmates.

i hope on your off days
i can make you more whole.
though i know i will never
be able to complete you,
i want to make you more complete
as you have me.

-false wholeness

he does not define your worth.
He defines your worth.

my other mother held my hands
and looked into my eyes
with hers full of tears.
she said what you are doing for others
is what He did
for us.
He lived fearlessly
and lovingly.
He was crucified.
humiliated,
and put to death
for you and me.
but He rose again.
baby girl,
you will
rise again.

-learning how to actually love

mary magdalene

i have no clue
no idea
no concept
no vision
about half of my heritage,
while the other half
i see
is diagnosed with
numerous mental illnesses
and strung out on drugs.
you pressure and expect me
to identify myself
and know who i want to be
with such little context.
all they have shown me
and made me sure about
is what i do not
want for myself
and my own
future family.

-unknown genetics and heritage

my mother wishes to be someone else
when others criticize her
calling her
an unfit mother.
they only see what they want to.
i have to pity them too
and assume the slits in their eyes
are as narrow as their minds.
because the chemicals in my mother's brain
caused by men who viewed her as a bank
where they kept and stole
her treasure
for pleasure,
it is their actions that have resulted in the pain.
she never prayed to be that woman,
but now she feels like she cannot be anyone else.

as an orphan my mother was in the wrong places
at the wrong times,
trying to gain resources to raise her baby brother
while enduring the trauma of losing parents
at such a young age.
she was only doing what she thought was best.

my mother is not unfit
as her daughter i cannot even fully understand
her sorrows,
so when you place judgments on my mother,
i hurt for you
for it must not be your fault
that your perspectives are a grain of salt.
and my mother is as vast as the ocean,

so i will remember not to blame you for your
misunderstanding.
something so beautiful can never completely
be understood.
what is vast
can never fully be seen,
but it can be loved
and forgiven for the sharks that swim in it.
for the ocean did not ask for sea monsters,
the environment is just fitting for them.

-blind outsiders attempting to look in

i can only expect so much from a woman
who already had everything good
robbed from her.

Jesus called his disciples over and said, "The truth is
that this poor widow gave more to the collection than
all the others put together. All the others gave what
they'll never miss; she gave extravagantly what she
couldn't afford—she gave her all."
Mark 12:41-44

3 things my mother taught me:

1. real life lessons are often learned in unconventional manners.

   my mom did not have many opportunities to show me what i could or should be, but from her, i learned i did not want poverty for my own family. i understand there are two kinds of poverties: the one you experience when you are made fun of at school, because you have to go to the church food bank where your classmates' parents work; and the kind when your mom never showed up to your sporting events because she was hustlin' so the kids at school would not make fun of her daughter anymore.

2. sacrifice looks different for everyone.

   to the same women who raise their noses to my mother and say she is not sacrificial: you do not know what sacrifice looks like in all of its forms.

   my mother carried me for nine months and chose to give me life after being raped. my mother sacrificed numbness and dealt with the pain all over again when she gave up drugs after finding out i lived inside her womb. my mother sacrificed her dignity when she posed to

take pictures and spread her legs for men
who would make sure there was a roof
over our heads.

3. prayer is powerful.

my mother told me she prayed for victory
and a prosperous future for me. she
named me victoria hope and spoke that
over me my entire life. God heard my
mother and answered her prayers.

when i get my hair done i get to step into the part of my culture i know very little about. an aspect of me that is usually predominantly pointed out as different is not even acknowledged. i am simply same. i get to talk to women who know more about my faceless biological father than i ever will. they have not met him either, but i understand more about him and his absence as i listen to their stories. the most ironic part may be as i talk to them i am reminded of my beautiful, loud, vivacious, and sacrificial biological mother. i assume it is because even though they laugh while telling stories of adversity and though i can see their smile lines, i recognize the same wrinkles caused by pain that also rest on my mother's stunning face. here, we do not get our hair done. here, i sat with queens as we got our crowns polished.

my mother always told me
"your hair is your crown."
and since rebellion
runs through my veins
i chopped it all off
until there was barely any left.
i've learned many lessons
by doing what i "shouldn't"
or "couldn't"
do.
including that one-
something about
regardless of the length or style
of a woman's hair,
she's always a queen.
and there is no crown
or title
or physical image
that trumps the character of
a heroine that creates peace,
a monarch rebuilding what is broken,
a ruler willing to serve her people,
a woman
who wears unconditional
and sacrificial
love
as her crown.

*...hair is a crown of splendor; it is attained in the way
of righteousness.*
Proverbs 16:31

one of my greatest fears
is that i will end up
just like my mother -
wearing mink coats
of desperate forgiveness
on hot summer days
begging cold men
to keep me warm.

my mother is the goddess of fertility.
i floated in her dead sea
for nine months,
so when i found myself
in the deep waters
in the gulf of aden,
i had no trepidation.
i knew how to swim.
and when i stepped onto the holy ground,
i could walk alone.

-strong women breed stronger women

my family was broken
all the time.
nonexistent
most times.
changing about every
six months.
i just wanted
to make a perfect
family of my own.
take all of the shattered
pieces from my own
and glue them back
together to create
something that could never
be cracked.
but my religion and culture
says i cannot do this alone.
and as i witness my single mother
struggle
i would have to agree
that the fear of raising
a precious life alone
cripples me.

i take a second glance
at my mother.
or maybe i am looking
at my own reflection.
i will make a home
out of no one.
i am fully capable of
creating a miracle of my own
as she created me.

but she was forced
in a dirty home
with meth in his sweat
dripping on her body
and cocaine in his sperm
that mixed with my mothers
egg
to manifest the miracle
that is me.

i have the choice to patiently
wait.
my mom made a home for me
when she did not have to.
so i will take the time
to make a home
for me
so someday i can be a home
for my own my offspring.

a woman is a womb.
called to receive
as Jesus received God.
we receive semen
and create something new
and beautiful of it.
and we are called to
receive Christ
and bear God
to the world.
we are the vessel.
this is our dignity.
this is our calling.

confessions of the fostered

my mind cannot rest.
nor can my mind focus
on what is in front of me,
as it forms words and memories,
of everything
i want in front of me.
you are everything.

break
when weak.
i am supposed to be strong,
but my goodness,
you make me weak.
you can shatter my day.
and you can put it back together.
you can make tears
roll down my face
harder than the fierce
waterfalls in the mountains.
you can make me feel on top
and you can make me feel so low.
you can make me feel
brighter than the sun
on the clearest days.
you have a power to crush,
shatter,
and break me,
so please,
be cautious.
and take good care of me.

foster care forces you
to move on.
it makes you question
if you are even capable of loving.
every time you are ripped
out of another place
that was supposed to be
home
and moved to another people
that you are supposed to call
family,
though in approximately
six months they would
decide you are not worth
the hassle
or even the money.

you have learned to love
every kind of person.
you see everyone is
the way they are for a reason.
you find yourself falling
you are always falling
in love
with the idea of having a unit
love you forever.
no matter what.

until the part of you that is
your biological mother peeks
her head from the darkness
and makes eye contact with
your foster mother.

then you beg your foster father
to convince her to let you stay,
you apologize and beg them
to never leave.
to see that your worth is
beyond this moment.
but through the moves
even when it is all your fault
you had to move on.
there was always something
inside of you screaming
"you are not the victim.
you are the victor."
when you live in a home
with ten other children
you don't get much attention or love.
but you still
pray this will be the last home
and the forever family.
you learn you have to love
everything you don't like
regardless if this is a good fit
because you cannot fathom
the idea
of more humans
leaving.

the system taught me
how to love every kind of person
under the moon.

but when all you are seeking is
foreverness and unconditional love
stability and a hope so deep
it can wrestle with your biggest dreams
you forget that not everyone can love
like you.
and you search for the same thing
in a man
as you did in every family.
regardless of the abuse,
and neglect,
you hold on,
because you cannot handle
another move.
i cannot not watch
one more human
leave me.

mini sermon: fulfillment through love

there is no man on this earth that can fulfill what
your father did not give you. there is no home or
family that can replace the one you did not have.
do not go making a home in any human. the new
man who came to save you from that heartbreak
will not be able to find your heart, pick it up, put
it back together, all while searching for the tools
to place it back in your chest. i do not advise you
to trust any earthly man; and i'm not saying this
because "all men are the same." it is because all
men are human, as you are, and only God can fix
something as tattered and torn and broken as us.

loving yourself probably seems impossible to
even begin. sometimes when i feel unlovable, i
can't help but look at all of the people who left. if
people loved me and cared about me, why
wouldn't they have stayed? and as time has gone
on, i have realized i have needed to experience
new people and new love and new life at different
times in my life to be who i am today. some
people needed to go and new needed to enter. i
had to experience something different to be
prepared for the next adventure God wanted to
take me on.

and most importantly, by being loved by so many
different people and loving so many others, i can
see God glisten in different people's heart. i can
love anyone, because i can see God in everyone.

that precious china
you thought was unbreakable
shatters all over the floor.
but it's okay
because you can put anything back together.
you're sure.
and as you finally get to look
at what you believe is the finished product,
a sigh of relief.
it appears better than ever before.
until you realize,
as you see the imprints of those shattered pieces
in someone else's soft hands,
you gave someone else this chore.
so you kiss those bleeding hands and
you vow to not do that anymore.
you realize this is your dish to fix,
because putting something so broken in the
hands of another,
just made it more fragile
than it had ever been before.

you only get a glimpse of a word
even when you are forced
to define it.

church hurt

church
community
family
we need one another
we need to bind
we are stronger together
but you left me alone
and deserted me
and chose others.
i'm not family.
i never have been
to anyone.
this was all a joke.
this is just a marketing hoax.
good thing i'm really good
at being alone.

mini sermon: Christ dwells in our souls

i was hiking saint mary's glacier in denver, colorado and a man asked me "tori, what is the soul?" i had spent years in college wrestling with this idea and questioning if the soul was even real. no one had asked me this since i decided what my answer was. so i was excited to answer him. i am excited to tell you.

i believe the soul is Christ living inside of every individual. even those people who have not yet accepted or come to know Christ are made in God's image; therefore, they have Christ in them. challenge yourself to explore your soul and dive deep into others'. it is through this, you will come to know a God who dwells inside of your very being.

i am too much
and at the same time i am never enough.
i am too loud
but i have a fear to speak up.
you cannot see all of my reactions,
because i am a contradiction.
i want you to see all of me
but i like to hide.
i am overly confident,
because i am trembling in anxiety.
you could not even begin to understand,
because you say you do
just too quickly.

i notice it.
i get it.
after my mother told me
i was a spitting image of my
rapist
drug addict
coward of a
father,
and after living a life
cautious of being just like my
bipolar
volatile
abusive
schizophrenic
mother,
i have no problem
seeing the bad in myself.
you don't have to point it out.

go to counseling
figure it out
become better
because you're never good enough
and you never will be.
you never have been
and you never will be.
so go talk about all of the bad parts of your life
and have someone tell you it's not your fault.
tell them the triggers that come from it
and who caused them.
so they can tell you about all the tricks
you've always tried
and you'll make a new discovery.
you're even more broken than everyone initially
thought.
there's no psychiatric glue or insecurity eraser
strong enough
to put you together and make you whole.
you can't be fixed.

he silenced me for so long
so now when it is my turn
to speak
i question the value of my words.
my voice shakes
through unsure words.
i wish i knew what to say.
please be patient
as i take back my voice,
from the man who never
deserved to hear me
utter a word.

i kept telling myself
"this is the best thing that's ever happened.
this the happiest thing on earth."
but i knew it would go away,
because everything good in my life disappears
and anything good
is the last thing i deserve.

my loudest & longest opinion:
the pro-life-Christian-conservative's
contradiction

i was conceived out of rape. when my mother was
upset with me she would tell me i was the spitting
image of a rapist. i will never forget sitting in the
passenger seat of a green pick-up truck, my mother
was driving me to school through the morning fog.
outraged and embarrassed that she had to sign
another pink-slip, because i had failed yet another
math test in the sixth grade, my mom screamed, her
eyes full of tears, "you are just a rape product." my
life was not valued or celebrated by my mother
because of the way i was conceived, especially
during times such as these.

despite my former beliefs regarding atheism and my
poor ideas about what freedom is, i always stood
pro-life. i believe every life deserves to be
celebrated despite how, when, or what brought the
child into the world. i have always been grateful my
mother chose to birth me and grant me life.
although life has been difficult at times, i am
thankful for the life i have had. By the grace of
God, i have received several messages and met with
many people who have shared that my story has
changed their lives for the better. God has taken a
hurtful start and redeemed it. i am constantly
baffled by the opportunities i have been granted, the
gifts i have received, and the people i have met
because of the beautiful testimony God has granted

me. no woman should face what my mother did and no child should be diminished for being conceived by rape, born into poverty, born out of wedlock, and so on- every child deserves a celebration at conception and forevermore, for God's plans for that child is beyond our comprehension.

this is ultimately the pro-life argument. life starts at conception, yet women kill their own children. rather than celebrating life, women become buried in fear, covered in despair, and wallow in shame. i truly believe anyone who advocates for a woman to freely choose murdering her innocent, unborn, dependent, worthy, and loved baby is the poorest of the poor. politically, i like to think i remain moderate, but in this case i am unashamedly on the same side as the majority of conservatives.

though i have been involved and met many people involved in pro-life movements, dedicated to defund abortions, reaching out to scared women facing unexpected pregnancies, offering countless resources for babies, mothers, and families, and saving baby human's lives, i have recently witnessed a significant contradiction in the pro-life-christian-conservatives' "movement to end abortion."

while attending the school considered "the most conservative college in the nation," and being close to several different Christian families, sharing my out-of-wedlock pregnancy with people i was closest to and my various communities resulted in much discouragement. i knew i had sinned. i knew my sin was on display and i knew i had work to do to draw myself back to God, forgiveness to seek, and repentance to exemplify; but i did not expect the reactions received. the first words out of different [conservative and Christian] people's mouths were "we will have to process this." and "this is going to be so hard." and "you have lost so much of your life so early." i lost many friends very quickly, i was harassed, i felt alone, full of shame, embarrassed to celebrate because people told me they deserved my remorse. usually when women announce pregnancies to their families and friends, hugs and laughing take place. i experienced distancing and tears. i always found glory and joy while dreaming about being a mother and having my own family, but after hearing these voices and words repeat in my head, i promptly became too apologetic to celebrate. though I am grateful for celebrations that came later, it reminded me and left me disappointed that i will never get the chance to celebrate the beginning of my family and the genesis of my first born, as many women do, ever again.

many conservatives outwardly express pro-life beliefs, but only if the child comes into the world on their terms-morally, with stability, and definite security. i am not naive about the financial and emotional struggles my husband and i will encounter as we tackle parenthood, but i know our lives have not diminished, but rather enhanced as we have been chosen and blessed to create life. and i believe this about all women who conceive a child no matter what the circumstances.

i believe conservatives and pro-lifers should improve their tactics. i am not denying the evidence. there is plenty of research proving that getting pregnant while financially and mentally stable in a marriage often results in healthy lives and stability while raising children; but if pro-lifers rhetoric is "this is going to be so hard" to an immature, poor, unmarried, yet educated, employed, couple who loves each other deeply, how can anyone expect a single woman who grew up without a father, a woman who lives in poverty, or a woman who was raped to be convinced that having a child is "the greatest gift?" why have a baby when the people who are offering you resources are saying "this is going to be so hard" while in tears? why value a life when even the people who "value life" express fear and defer shame upon women who have created life outside of a fixed and fastened spectrum? we must ask ourselves these questions, as pro-lifers, to eliminate contradictions in our beliefs, our expressions, and our actions. and we must change our rhetoric to love and understanding, because the value of life, God's plan for the conceived, and pro-life is 100% and no exceptions from the moment of conception.

i'll sit by myself
and i'll ask God for help
since i need it so badly
more than anyone else.
i've always been the most broken
and most lost among all men
so i'm going to raise my hands in surrender
and ask God to,
just this one more time,
put me back together again.

i have many talents.
you can ask him what they are.
he will say what i touch
turns into disaster.
i destroy everything wide and far.
i pray for God to help me
help others experience life
through Him,
but i'm nothing but a cause of death.
here i am,
dying all over again.

mini sermon: you are tasty fruit

reminding myself that i am made in God's image
always reminds me to love myself. don't get me
wrong. there are parts of me that i hate and i
want tossed away forever - that sin and pride and
insecurity and shame. but i can vow to love
myself every time i recognize the characteristics
of God, because i was created to obtain those
same characteristics, the fruits of the Him - love,
joy, peace, patience, kindness, goodness,
faithfulness, gentleness, and self-control. being
made in God's image means that through
recognizing His good works and His enduring
love and by believing that He lives in us, we can
be like Him. we are called to this. we are called to
love His creation, being ourselves.

*So God created mankind in his own image, in the image
of God he created them; male and female he created them.*
Genesis 1:27

we constructed a course,
and created a world,
with a wobbly foundation
and little resources.
we just didn't know,
but let's learn together.
there's no reason to go.
we can withstand this harsh weather.
and show each other what we can build
if we just do it for each other.

i will not make a home out of you.
i will not make a home out of you.
i will not make a home out of you.
God is my safe haven and home.

guard your heart.
guard your heart.
guard your heart.
because God is meant
to flow from it.

love like you won't get hurt.
love like you won't get hurt.
love like you won't get hurt.
because God loves us
regardless of the hurt.

i've never understood apathy,
because i only feel empathy.
deeply.
weeping.
seeking.
maybe a weakness,
but i wouldn't want
any other constant feeling,
because i know i am called
to understand and know
as much as humans have to show.
so if my eyes happen to close
i'll already have experienced
the faithfulness of God
through my own
and others highs and lows.

someone asked me how i carry on
so quickly after my dreams drown.
i told him i've become
used to people letting me down.
and when he looked into my eyes with a frown,
i said "it's not as bad as it sounds."
in actuality my dreams never drown.
if the dream was never meant to be,
it was never meant to be my dream.
i carry on because i see a gleam.
of hope.
i'll just continue to seek
whatever dream God has for me.

-drowning dreams

Our marriage & my healing

may you encounter
the God of compassion
 in the unexpected,
the disrupted,
and at the margins.
 may you know,
without a doubt, that you are right
where you are supposed to be.

before You came along
i was killing people.
and i was in the process of
killing myself
with the words i spoke to others
and with the lies i told myself.
You have given so many people
new life
because of the way You speak to me
when You lift me up
encourage me
and declare the good
in my soul.
i have been able to do
for so many others
only because You did it for me.

-the domino effect of speaking life

this generation keeps
referring to themselves as "the fatherless."
but I'm right here.
protecting.
sheltering.
loving.
I'm not like your earthly father.
I'll prove it to you as we go.
just keep your eyes open.
I made myself harder to see
only for the sake that your trust
would be greater in Me.
but I'm right here.

*No temptation has overtaken you except what is
common to mankind. And God is faithful; he
will not let you be tempted beyond what you can
bear. But when you are tempted, he will also
provide a way out so that you can endure it.
1 Corinthians 10:13*

i have a few forever homes now.
i am happy to have more than one.
it is crazy to think at one point i had none.
my First Home will also be my last.
but i have a few settlings before i make it there.
the perk of settling with you,
is that you'll let me bring my First Home,
no compromise,
because it is already yours.
and as i lay in our future home
and i think of the space you will make
i know it is you,
who is my next home.
and with Him already as our home.
i rest unafraid of the winds that may blow
and the storms that will come,
because we have a Home
that nothing could destroy.
so i rejoice in what God has created
and i will embrace you as
home sweet home.

mini sermon: comfort

oftentimes, when we think, of comfort, we think of squishy and kind or soft and gentle feelings. in latin, the root word, "com" means "together and "fort" means "strength." comfort joins us together with community, with family, and if that is something you feel like you do not have, comfort always joins you with Christ. therefore, it only makes you stronger. just because you need comfort, doesn't mean you are weak. you are strong through Christ. you are recognizing that strength in yourself and committing to making it stronger through your love for others and faith in God. join me in comfort. join Christ. He is already dwelling in You and He only wants you to feel comfort through His love, in a relationship with Him.

May your unfailing love be my comfort,
according to your promise to your servant.
Psalm 119:76

hummingbird moths
seem darker and dangerous
on the outside,
but they have a spirit
of a hummingbird.
wings tattered and torn.
though they hum,
and drink honeyed flowers,
and sing to us.
they draw close.
like the Holy Spirit,
Who makes us safe and peaceful
on the inside.
He grants us a spirit
of a hummingbird,
though our wings
are tattered and torn.
we hear a hum
in his whispers.
we drink from a fountain
of honey He supplies.
we sing to Him praises.
we draw close.

Draw near to God and He will draw near to you.
James 4:8

God saved me when i was seventeen years old.
and He has saved me every day since.
He is the only man i have encountered
that still loves me at all my mess.

my sweet child,
I have come to you
as your Father.
take a breather
and believe in Me.
I will show you,
you are more loved
than you could ever imagine.
you won't experience it in this world.
because I am not of this world.
and I am calling you to more.
so take My hand, daughter.
and let me show you,
above all else,
you are Mine.

The Spirit you received does not make you slaves, so that you live in fear again; rather, the Spirit you received brought about your adoption to sonship. And by him we cry, "Abba, Father."
Romans 8:15

i am going to build a home out of you.
not so i can live in it
but so you can feel built up.
i'll be your sturdy structure.
i can be your unbreakable bedrock.

-just offer me the tools so we can construct

stifle your pride.
stop trying to be the tough guy.
God, the strongest man alive,
humbled Himself, willing to die.
and you roll your eyes.
when i say i'll die
to my desires
my forever and enduring cries
are to throw those evil parts of me
in the fires.
but i will need you to patiently wait,
as i walk towards heavenly gates.
because i'll never be perfect,
but i'll always strive towards it.
so hold on, don't leave quite yet.
please don't walk away from me.
just keep your heart and eyes open
ready to see.
God is trying to set
the beautiful, captive parts
Satan has captured free.

*Now the Lord is the Spirit, and where the Spirit of the
Lord is, there is freedom.*
2 Corinthians 3:17

the maternal instinct as a woman
is to hug, care, and nurture
whatever is crazy
and screaming
and crying
and flailing.
to calm
and heal
and soothe
back to peace
whatever is hurting.
we must first learn
to do it for ourselves
before we do it for someone
more vulnerable,
more malleable,
and more fragile
than ourselves.

God created *Christian* men
to be the headship of women.
so if a man tells you to follow him,
to see if he is right,
you assess and analyze his life.
to have a beautiful woman like yourself,
committed and unconditionally loving,
willing to follow and be by his side,
you must be absolutely sure,
he is relentlessly devoted and following Christ.

*But I want you to understand that the head of every
man is Christ, the head of a wife is her husband, and
the head of Christ is God.*
1 Corinthians 11:3

"what was it like to meet him?" asked redemption.
"it's been storming for so long. the thunder is loud, but after years of crying out and not being heard, everything is suddenly calm enough for me to be understood and for me to understand this storm and see the rainbow." i said.
"what is it like to love him?" asked peace
"a storm surrounds me but i am sitting on dry, soft grass in the warm sunlight as a soft breeze kisses my skin." i replied
"what is it like to be loved by him?" asked joy.
"under the most beautiful rainbow, the sun shines. the drops gently touch my skin as soft as his hands graze my waist as i dance in the rain." i explained.
"what was it like when he stayed?" asked faithfulness.
"i know i will endure many storms, some harsher than the ones before; but i know i will never have to withstand the storms alone."

-the blessing of an earthly husband

i will need you to continue
to remind me
that you are not him.
and as i come to know
this to be true
through your relentless
loving actions,
i will try my absolute best
to make you not suffer
the consequences
of their dilapidation.

-trying again

reminder to self:
any other rock
i attempt to stand on,
will crumble.
i want to be so grounded
in God
so i stop throwing away
my gifts
and deserting Him
every time something new
comes around.
why have i not learned the lesson?
if i am not in Him,
secure and stable,
i lose my balance.
i fall.
i lose myself.
because i lose who
He wants me to be.
as i accept conditional love
and reject
His unconditional love.

*The LORD is my rock, my fortress and my deliverer; my
God is my rock, in whom I take refuge, my shield and the
horn of my salvation, my stronghold.*
Psalm 18:2

if we have certainty
we have lost our hope and faith.
we don't seek knowledge.
we seek hope
because if we obtain all knowledge
we do not need hope.

tangled in soft sheets
and softer skin
you touched my body
and prayed over it.
mumbling praise for what
had been disgraced
and whispering truths
into pores filled with falsehoods.
no one had ever touched me
as tender as you did then.
after that night
i was sure God healed me
while i was wrapped in your skin.

-marital

how much art
will we make with these wrists
and how many babies
will we hold with these arms
and how many tears
will we wipe with these hands
and how many prayers
will we speak on these knees
and how many victories
will we celebrate
lowly and humbly
standing firm on these feet.

-conception

you are broken.
and so is he.
and so is she.
and so is everyone.
you're not alone.
but hold on
that's not all I want you to see.
I can show you more.
you are not just a shattered heart.
let Me pick you up off of that dirty floor.
you are a piece of art.
I want to convince you.
just let Me intercede.
I want to experience
an agape love with you.
it's all you'll ever need.

Just as the Father has loved Me, I have also loved you;
abide in My love.
John 15:9

you dislike most things society.
you embrace counterculture.
and like me, you also have
the most rebellious of rebel hearts.
your opinions are louder than mine.
you don't ask me to be meek.
and when we have confrontation
you don't back down
because you know better
than to treat me
like i'm weak.

but sometimes i'm weak.
and you put your strength
and robust opinions
to the side.
to put me up front.
your voice gets as soft as the blankets
i wrap myself in at night.
and you wrap me in your arms.
your touch gets more gentle
and your words drench me in comfort.
i remember your promises
are as true as human promises
can be.

because you dislike everything
out of the norm.
you are the kind of man
our culture has shunned and banned

i'm happy.
i'm fine.
i'm not left behind.
i want to believe.
i want to see
life as bright
as the sunrise.

From the rising of the sun to its setting The name of the
LORD is to be praised.
Psalm 113:3

God reminded me of who i was.
sometimes i miss the whole scope.
and God reminded me
of who He made me to be.
i am grounded in new hope.
He helps me see
and understand more of this story.
i can do anything through Him.
for He is the reason i conquer
and experience victory.

For the LORD your God is the one who goes with you
to fight for you against your enemies to give you
victory.
Deuteronomy 20:4

the questioning:
i wonder "where did this come from?"
"what was its original purpose?"
"how much time was put into it?"
"how difficult was it to create?"
"is there more than one?"
"is this the original?"
i wonder, "where did i originate from?"
"what was the purpose behind my creation?"
"did i have one?"
"how much time and thought was put
into the creation of me?"
"could there be another one of me somewhere
else?"

the realization:
i was born of two drug addicts
diagnosed with bipolar and schizophrenia,
in the hood of houston, texas.
there was no plan for me to be here.
my sperm donor wanted pleasure.
my mother wanted to be numb.
no one thought about me.
i was not supposed to exist.
there may be more of me
from the same man.
this may just be what he does.
i probably am not the first.

the awakening:
i originated in the hands of God.
the same God who created the sun
that can grant energy

to every living creature.
in the womb my purpose
was to heal my mother-
to make her purer than she
has ever been
through a cleanse.
my purpose has become
to glorify God
by loving people
in some capacity.
because i was made
in the image of God.
this is how He thought of me.
though my earthly father
does not know i exist
this is how my Heavenly Father knows me.
it is a mystery
that i was meant to exist.
as He is a mystery that exist.

so much has changed.
almost everything.
yet i am more me
than i ever have been.

Your love is a flood,
but even as the waves hit me,
i am staying afloat.
i can swim,
fast, strong, and swift.
i want to stay in this Deep Water.

Many waters cannot quench love; rivers cannot sweep it
away. If one were to give all the wealth of one's house
for love, it would be utterly scorned.
Song of Solomon 8:7

arrive at day seven.
and to come rest.
I want you to
experience some heaven.
on earth,
this was not a test.
just your rebirth.
never second guess,
darling, you must always believe
I am only doing what is best.

By the seventh day God had finished the work he had
been doing; so on the seventh day he rested from all his
work.
Genesis 2:2

when no one is listening,
when there is not enough time
to process,
and there is no energy
to be heard,
talk to the flowers.
as a reminder
that no matter how different
when compared to another,
beauty is obtained
and remains.
while being quiet,
they'll stay,
no matter what you say.
only moving,
doing so gently,
when the wind blows.
knowing their roots
will endure the weather,
reflecting steady growth and life.

The grass withers, the flower fades, But the word of our God stands forever.
Isaiah 40:8

men are like lightning.
rather momentary.
and then we hear the rumbling
the shaking and shattering thunder.
it moves the entire world.
as the woman extends the storm
when she was created
and then again as she bears a child.
this life carries on God's glory.
and makes the church.
without women there would not be
a perfect storm.

God's love is a medicine of peace
i get to take.
the sweetest aroma i experience
for my own sake.
the strongest glue
i use
to put my broken-self back together.
the best advice.
so gentle, clear, and concise.
the least expensive rubber eraser
that makes insecurity disappear.
then the piece of paper is clearer
to reflect on who He is
and who we are
because we are made in His image.
He is so loving,
without us having to pay any primage
He made us like Him.

For God so loved the world, that he gave his only Son,
that whoever believes in him should not perish but have
eternal life
John 3:16

God's creation - mountains.
only the most powerful weather
causes them to erode.
formed through falling.
yet they stand strong through storms.
their beauty remains regardless;
and when The Light shines upon them,
their glory is only exemplified.
and we are reminded of
God's creation - you.

*How beautiful on the mountains are the feet of those
who bring good news, who proclaim peace, who bring
good tidings, who proclaim salvation, who say to Zion,
"Your God reigns!"*
Isaiah 52:7

your spirit has wings
made of glitter.
and every time you choose to fly,
you graciously allow others
to see that glimmer.

but those who hope in the LORD will renew their
strength. They will soar on wings like eagles; they will
run and not grow weary, they will walk and not be
faint.
Isaiah 40:31

i can't tell you
i love you
because i don't speak your language,
 but you remind me that love is a hug.
love is a hand to hold.
it is blowing bubbles.
it is dancing under the sunshine
 and doing whatever possible
to make you smile.
love is a choice and an action.

-foreign mission

speak to me.
I'm listening.
you could never talk too much.
you're not too much.
oh, beautiful.
the time I spend with you,
it's actually never enough.
you are not a disappointment, daughter.
I made myself human so I could understand you.
and as you hurt, I'm hurting too.
I have experienced your pain.
I know suffering all too well.
I will wash away that shame.
I'll hold onto the secrets that you tell.
thank you for your honesty.
I still love you
and I always will.

*This is the confidence we have in approaching God:
that if we ask anything according to His will, He hears
us.*
1 John 5:14

with Me there's no such thing as abandonment.
experience the sacrament.
this is a covenant.

*Peter said to them, "Repent, and each of you be
baptized in the name of Jesus Christ for the forgiveness
of your sins; and you will receive the gift of the Holy
Spirit.*
Acts 2:38

roses have been planted in my heart.
occasionally those roses don't grow.
at times they only get as far as a bud
before they fall onto the ground.
my hopes rise
as the the roses begin to grow
tall and healthy.
i strive
to keep them alive.
i learn how to take care
of the beautiful plants
that began as seeds
God planted in my heart.
then disappointment overwhelms me
as they wilt.
lifeless and dead roses
are scattered and covering every surface.
so i start over.
new seeds are planted.
and i use my failures as lessons.
some days i have a rose garden.
some days i have soil
that looks like it's never been toiled
or rained on.
but because of God
there are always seeds
planted in my heart.

*You visit the earth and cause it to overflow; You greatly
enrich it; The stream of God is full of water; You
prepare their grain, for thus You prepare the earth.
Psalm 65:9*

believe Me,
My love is hesed and agape,
unlike anything else.
it is in your heart.
I want it to breakthrough.
because I know many have spoken these words
as a lie.
but My covenant is true.
I solemnly swear, you do not have to doubt.
I will never leave you
nor forsake you.

Be strong and courageous. Do not be afraid or terrified
because of them, for the LORD your God goes with
you; he will never leave you nor forsake you. "
Deuteronomy 31:6

22483642R00075

Made in the USA
Lexington, KY
14 December 2018